CW00551114

**William Dean Howells**

# A Likely Story

**William Dean Howells**

# A Likely Story

1st Edition | ISBN: 978-3-75237-513-8

Place of Publication: Frankfurt am Main, Germany

Year of Publication: 2020

Outlook Verlag GmbH, Germany.

# A LIKELY STORY

BY
## W. D. HOWELLS

# I

# MR. AND MRS. WILLIS CAMPBELL

Mrs. Campbell: "Now this, I think, is the most exciting part of the whole affair, and the pleasantest." She is seated at breakfast in her cottage at Summering-by-the-Sea. A heap of letters of various stylish shapes, colors, and superscriptions lies beside her plate, and irregularly straggles about among the coffee-service. Vis-à-vis with her sits Mr. Campbell behind a newspaper. "How prompt they are! Why, I didn't expect to get half so many answers yet. But that shows that where people have nothing to do *but* attend to their social duties they are always prompt—even the men; women, of course, reply early anyway, and you don't really care for them; but in town the men seem to put it off till the very last moment, and then some of them call when it's over to excuse themselves for not having come after accepting. It really makes you wish for a leisure class. It's only the drive and hurry of American life that make our men seem wanting in the *convenances*; and if they had the time, with their instinctive delicacy, they would be perfect: it would come from the heart: they're more truly polite now. Willis, just *look* at this!"

Campbell, behind his paper: "Look at what?"

Mrs. Campbell: "These replies. Why, I do believe that more than half the people have answered already, and the invitations only went out yesterday. That comes from putting on R.S.V.P. I knew I was right, and I shall always do it, I don't care what *you* say."

Campbell: "You didn't put on R.S.V.P. after all I said?" He looks round the edge of his paper at her.

Mrs. Campbell: "*Yes*, I did. The idea of your setting up for an authority in such a thing as that!"

Campbell: "Then I'm sorry I didn't ask you to do it. It's a shame to make people say whether they'll come to a garden-party from four till seven or not."

Mrs. Campbell: "A shame? How can you provide if you don't know how many are coming? I should like to know that. But of course I couldn't expect you to give in gracefully."

Campbell: "I should give in gracefully if I gave in at all, but I don't." He throws his paper down beside his chair. "Here, hand over the letters, and I'll be opening them for you while you pour out the coffee."

Mrs. Campbell, covering the letters with her hands: "Indeed you won't!"

Campbell: "Well, pour out the coffee, then, anyway."

Mrs. Campbell, after a moment's reflection: "No, I shall not do it. I'm going to open them every one before you get a drop of coffee—just to punish you."

Campbell: "To punish me? For what?" Mrs. Campbell hesitates, as if at a loss what to say. "There! you don't know."

Mrs. Campbell: "Yes, I do: for saying I oughtn't to have put on R.S.V.P. Do you take it back?"

Campbell: "How can I till I've had some coffee? My mind won't work on an empty stomach. Well—" He rises and goes round the table towards her.

Mrs. Campbell, spreading both arms over the letters: "Willis, if you dare to touch them, I'll ring for Jane, and then she'll see you cutting up."

Campbell: "Touch what? I'm coming to get some coffee."

Mrs. Campbell: "Well, I'll give you some coffee; but don't you touch a single one of those letters—after what you've said."

Campbell: "All right!" He extends one hand for the coffee, and with the other sweeps all the letters together, and starts back to his place. As she flies upon him, "Look out, Amy; you'll make me spill this coffee all over the table-cloth."

Mrs. Campbell, sinking into her seat: "Oh, Willis, how can you be so base? *Give* me my letters. *Do!*"

Campbell, sorting them over: "You may have half."

Mrs. Campbell: "No; I shall have all. I insist upon it."

Campbell: "Well, then, you may have all the ladies' letters. There are twice as many of them."

Mrs. Campbell: "No; I shall have the men's, too. Give me the men's first."

Campbell: "How can I tell which are the men's without opening them?"

Mrs. Campbell: "How could you tell which were the ladies'? Come, now, Willis, don't tease me any longer. You know I hate it."

Campbell, studying the superscriptions, one after another: "I want to see if I can guess who wrote them. Don't you like to guess who wrote your letters before you open them?"

Mrs. Campbell, with dignity: "I don't like to guess who wrote other people's letters." She looks down at the table-cloth with a menace of tears, and Campbell instantly returns all the notes.

Campbell: "There, Amy; you may have them. I don't care who wrote them, nor what's in them. And I don't want you to interrupt me with any exclamations over them, if you please." He reaches to the floor for his newspaper, and while he sips his coffee, Mrs. Campbell loses no time in opening her letters.

Mrs. Campbell: "I shall do nothing *but* exclaim. The Curwens accept, of course—the very first letter. That means Mrs. Curwen; that is one, at any rate. The New York Addingses do, and the Philadelphia Addingses don't; I hardly expected they would, so soon after their aunt's death, but I thought I ought to ask them. Mr. and Mrs. Roberts, naturally; it was more a joke than anything, sending their invitation. Mrs. and the Misses Carver regret very much; well, *I* don't. Professor and Mrs. Traine are very happy, and so am I; he doesn't go everywhere, and he's awfully nice. Mr. and Mrs. Lou Bemis are very happy, too, and Dr. Lawton is very happy. Mrs. Bridges Dear Mrs. Campbells me, and is very sorry in the first person; she's always nice. Mr. Phillips, Mr. Rangeley, Mr. Small, Mr. Peters, Mr. Staples, Mr. Thornton, *all* accept, and they're all charming young fellows."

Campbell, around his paper: "Well, what of that?"

Mrs. Campbell, with an air of busy preoccupation: "Don't eavesdrop, please; I wasn't talking to you. The Merrills have the pleasure, and the Morgans are sorrow-stricken; the—"

Campbell: "Yes, but why should you care whether those fellows are charming or not? Who's going to marry them?"

Mrs. Campbell: "*I* am. Mrs. Stevenson is bowed to the earth; Colonel Murphree is overjoyed; the Misses Ja—"

Campbell, putting his paper down: "Look here, Amy. Do you know that you have one little infinitesimal ewe-lamb of a foible? You think too much of young men."

Mrs. Campbell: "*Younger* men, you mean. And *you* have a multitude of perfectly mammoth peccadilloes. You interrupt." She goes on opening and reading her letters. "Well, I didn't expect the Macklines *could*; but everybody seems to be coming."

Campbell: "You pay them too much attention altogether. It spoils them; and one of these days you'll be getting some of them in love with you, and *then* what will you do?"

Mrs. Campbell, with affected distraction: "What *are* you talking about? I'd refer them to you, and you could kill them. I suppose you killed lots of people in California. That's what you always gave me to understand." She goes on with her letters.

Campbell: "I never killed a single human being that I can remember; but there's no telling what I might do if I were provoked. Now, there's that young Welling. He's about here under my feet all the time; and he's got a way lately of coming in through the window from the piazza that's very intimate. He's a nice fellow enough, and sweet, as you say. I suppose he has talent, too, but I never heard that he had set any of the adjacent watercourses on fire; and I don't know that he could give the Apollo Belvedere many points in beauty and beat him."

Mrs. Campbell: "*I* do. Mrs. and Miss Rice accept, and her friend Miss Greenway, who's staying with her, and—yes! here's one from Mr. Welling! *Oh*, how glad I am! Willis, dearest, if I *could* be the means of bringing those two lovely young creatures together, I should be *so* happy! *Don't* you think, now, he *is* the most delicate-minded, truly refined, exquisitely modest young fellow that ever was?" She presses the unopened note to her corsage, and leans eagerly forward entreating a sympathetic acquiescence.

Campbell: "Well, as far as I can remember my own youth, no. But what does he say?"

Mrs. Campbell, regarding the letter: "I haven't looked yet. He writes the *most* characteristic hand, for a man, that I ever saw. And he has the divinest taste in perfumes! Oh, I wonder what *that* is? Like a memory—a regret." She presses it repeatedly to her pretty nose, in the endeavor to ascertain.

Campbell: "Oh, hello!"

Mrs. Campbell, laughing: "Willis, you *are* delightful. I should like to see you really jealous once."

Campbell: "You won't, as long as I know my own incomparable charm. But give me that letter, Amy, if you're not going to open it. I want to see whether Welling is going to come."

Mrs. Campbell, fondly: "Would you *really* like to open it? I've half a mind to let you, just for a reward."

Campbell: "Reward! What for?"

Mrs. Campbell: "Oh, I don't know. Being so nice."

Campbell: "That's something I can't help. It's no merit. Well, hand over the letter."

Mrs. Campbell: "I should have thought you'd insist on *my* opening it, after that."

Campbell: "Why?"

Mrs. Campbell: "To show your confidence."

Campbell: "When I haven't got any?"

Mrs. Campbell, tearing the note open: "Well, it's no use trying any sentiment with you, or any generosity either. You're always just the same; a teasing joke is your ideal. You can't imagine a woman's wanting to keep up a little romance all through; and a character like Mr. Welling's, who's all chivalry and delicacy and deference, is quite beyond you. That's the reason you're always sneering at him."

Campbell: "I'm not sneering at him, my dear. I'm only afraid Miss Rice isn't good enough for him."

Mrs. Campbell, instantly placated: "Well, she's the only girl who's anywhere *near* it. I don't say she's faultless, but she has a great deal of character, and she's very practical; just the counterpart of his dreaminess; and she *is* very, *very* good-looking, don't you think?"

Campbell: "Her bang isn't so nice as his."

Mrs. Campbell: "No; and aren't his eyes beautiful? And that high, serious look! And his nose and chin are perfectly divine. He looks like a young god!"

Campbell: "I dare say; though I never saw an old one. Well, is he coming? I'm not jealous, but I'm impatient. Read it out loud."

Mrs. Campbell, sinking back in her chair for the more luxurious perusal of the note: "Indeed I shall not." She opens it and runs it hastily through, with various little starts, stares, frowns, smiles of arrested development, laughs, and cries: "Why—why! What does it mean? Is he crazy? Why, there's some mistake. No! It's his hand—and here's his name. I can't make it out." She reads it again and again. "Why, it's perfectly bewildering! Why, there must be some mistake. He couldn't have meant it. Could he have imagined? Could he have dared? There never has been the slightest thing that could be tortured into—But of course not. And Mr. Welling, of all men! Oh, I can't understand it! Oh, Willis, Willis, Willis! What *does* it mean?" She flings the note wildly across the table, and catching her handkerchief to her face, falls back into her chair, tumultuously sobbing.

Campbell, with the calm of a man accustomed to emotional superabundance, lifting the note from the toast-rack before him: "Well, let's see." He reads aloud: "'Oh, my darling! How can I live till I see you? I will be there long *before* the hour! To think of your *asking* me! You should have said, "I permit you to come," and I would have flown from the ends of the earth. The presence of others will be nothing. It will be sweet to ignore them in my heart, and while I see you moving among them, and looking after their pleasure with that beautiful thoughtfulness of yours, to think, "She is mine, mine, mine!"

> "Oh, young lord lover, what sighs are those
> For one that can never be thine?"

I thank you, and thank you a thousand times over, for this proof of your trust in me, and of your love—*our* love. You shall be the sole keeper of our secret —it is so sweet to think that no one even suspects it!—and it shall live with you, and if you will, it shall die with me. Forever yours, Arthur Welling.'" Campbell turns the note over, and picking up the envelope, examines the address. "Well, *upon* my word! It's to you, Amy—on the outside, anyway. What do you suppose he means?"

Mrs. Campbell, in her handkerchief: "Oh, I don't know; I *don't* know why he should address such language to me!"

Campbell, recurring to the letter: "*I* never did. '*Oh, my darling—live till I see you—ends of the earth—others will be nothing—beautiful thoughtfulness—mine, mine, mine—our love—sweet to think no one suspects it—forever yours.*' Amy, these are pretty strong expressions to use towards the wife of another, and she a married lady! I think I had better go and solve that little problem of how he can live till he sees you by relieving him of the necessity. It would be disagreeable to him, but perhaps there's a social duty involved."

Mrs. Campbell: "Oh, Willis, *don't* torment me! What do you suppose it means? Is it some—mistake? It's for somebody else!"

Campbell: "I don't see why he should have addressed it to you, then."

Mrs. Campbell: "But don't you see? He's been writing to some other person at the same time, and he's got the answers mixed—put them in the wrong envelopes. Oh dear! I wonder who she is!"

Campbell, studying her with an air of affected abstraction: "Her curiosity gets the better of her anguish. Look here, Amy! *I* believe you're *afraid* it's to some one else."

Mrs. Campbell: "Willis!"

Campbell: "Yes. And before we proceed any further I must know just what you wrote to this—this Mr. Welling of yours. Did you put on R.S.V.P.?"

Mrs. Campbell: "Yes; and just a printed card like all the rest. I did want to write him a note in the first person, and urge him to come, because I expected

Miss Rice and Miss Greenway to help me receive; but when I found Margaret had promised Mrs. Curwen for the next day, I knew she wouldn't like to take the bloom off that by helping me first; so I didn't."

Campbell: "Didn't what?"

Mrs. Campbell: "Write to him. I just sent a card."

Campbell: "Then these passionate expressions *are* unprovoked, and my duty is clear. I must lose no time in destroying Mr. Welling. Do you happen to know where I laid my revolver?"

Mrs. Campbell: "Oh, Willis, what are you going to do? You see it's a mistake."

Campbell: "Mr. Welling has got to prove that. I'm not going to have young men addressing my wife as Oh their darling, without knowing the reason why. It's a liberty."

Mrs. Campbell, inclined to laugh: "Ah, Willis, how funny you are!"

Campbell: "Funny? I'm furious."

Mrs. Campbell: "You know you're not. Give me the letter, dearest. I know it's for Margaret Rice, and I shall see her, and just feel round and find out if it isn't so, and—"

Campbell: "What an idea! You haven't the slightest evidence that it's for Miss Rice, or that it isn't intended for you, and it's my duty to find out. And nobody is authority but Mr. Welling. And I'm going to him with the *corpus delicti*."

Mrs. Campbell: "But how can you? Remember how sensitive, how shrinking he is. Don't, Willis; you mustn't. It will kill him!"

Campbell: "Well, that may save me considerable bother. If he will simply die of himself, I can't ask anything better." He goes on eating his breakfast.

Mrs. Campbell, admiring him across the table: "Oh, Willis, how perfectly delightful you are!"

Campbell: "I know; but why?"

Mrs. Campbell: "Why, taking it in the nice, sensible way you do. Now, some husbands would be so stupid! Of course you *couldn't* think—you couldn't *dream*—that the letter was really for me; and yet you might behave very disagreeably, and make me very unhappy, if you were not just the lovely, kind-hearted, magnanimous—"

Campbell, looking up from his coffee: "Oh, hello!"

Mrs. Campbell: "Yes; that is what took my fancy in you, Willis: that generosity, that real gentleness, in spite of the brusque way you have. Refinement of the heart, *I* call it."

Campbell: "Amy, what are you after?"

Mrs. Campbell: "We've been married a whole year now—"

Campbell: "Longer, isn't it?"

Mrs. Campbell: "—And I haven't known you do an unkind thing, a brutal thing."

Campbell: "Well, I understand the banging around hardly ever begins much under two years."

Mrs. Campbell: "How *sweet* you are! And you're *so* funny always!"

Campbell: "Come, come, Amy; get down to business. What is it you do want?"

Mrs. Campbell: "You won't go and tease that poor boy about his letter, will you? Just hand it to him, and say you suppose here is something that has come into your possession by mistake, and that you wish to restore it to him, and then—just run off."

Campbell: "With my parasol in one hand, and my skirts caught up in the other?"

Mrs. Campbell: "Oh, how good! Of course I was imagining how *I* should do it."

Campbell: "Well, a man can't do it that way. He would look silly." He rises from the table, and comes and puts his arm round her shoulders. "But you needn't be afraid of my being rough with him. Of course it's a mistake; but he's a fellow who will enter into the joke too; he'll enjoy it; he'll—" He merges his sentence in a kiss on her upturned lips, and she clings to his hand with her right, pressing it fondly to her cheek. "I shall do it in a man's way; but I guess you'll approve of it quite as much."

Mrs. Campbell: "I know I shall. That's what I like about you, Willis: your being so helplessly a man always."

Campbell: "Well, that's what attracted me to you, Amy; your manliness."

Mrs. Campbell: "And I liked your *finesse*. You are awfully inventive, Willis. Why, Willis, I've just thought of something. Oh, it would be *so* good if you only would!"

Campbell: "Would what?"

Mrs. Campbell: "Invent something now to get us out of the scrape."

Campbell: "What a brilliant idea! *I'm* not in any scrape. And as for Mr. Welling, I don't see how you could help him out unless you sent this letter to Miss Rice, and asked her to send yours back—"

Mrs. Campbell, springing to her feet: "Willis, you are inspired! Oh, how perfectly delightful! And it's so delicate of you to think of that! I will just enclose his note—give it here, Willis—and he need never know that it ever went to the wrong address. Oh, I always felt that you were *truly* refined, anyway." He passively yields the letter, and she whirls away to a writing-desk in the corner of the room. "Now, I'll just keep a copy of the letter—for a joke; I think I've a perfect right to"—scribbling furiously away—"and then I'll match the paper with an envelope—I can do that perfectly—and then I'll just imitate his hand—such fun!—and send it flying over to Margaret Rice. Oh, *how* good! Touch the bell, Willis;" and then—as the serving-maid appears —"Yes, Jane! Run right across the lawn to Mrs. Rice's, and give this letter for Miss Margaret, and say it was left here by mistake. Well, it *was*, Willis. Fly, Jane! Oh, Willis, love! Isn't it perfect! Of course she'll have got his formal reply to my invitation, and be all mixed up by it, and now when this note comes, she'll see through it all in an instant, and it will be such a relief to her; and oh, she'll think that he's directed *both* the letters to her because he couldn't think of any one else! Isn't it lovely? Just like anything that's nice, it's ten times as nice as you expected it to be; and—"

Campbell: "But hold on, Amy!" He lifts a note from the desk. "You've sent your copy. Here's the original now. She'll think you've been playing some joke on her."

Mrs. Campbell, clutching the letter from him, and scanning it in a daze: "*What!* Oh, my goodness! It is! I have! Oh, I shall die! Run! Call her back! Shriek, Willis!" They rush to the window together. "No, no! It's too late! She's given it to their man, and now nothing can save me! Oh, Willis! Willis! Willis! This is all your fault, with that fatal suggestion of yours. Oh, if you had only left it to me I never should have got into such a scrape! She will think now that I've been trying to hoax her, and she's perfectly implacable at the least hint of a liberty, and she'll be ready to kill me. I don't know *what* she won't do. Oh, Willis, how *could* you get me into this!"

Campbell, irately: "Get you into this! Now, Amy, this is a little too much. You got yourself into it. You urged me to think of something—"

Mrs. Campbell: "Well, do, Willis, *do* think of something, or I shall go mad! Help me, Willis! Don't be so heartless—so unfeeling."

Campbell: "There's only one thing now, and that is to make a clean breast of it to Welling, and get him to help us out. A word from him can make everything right, and we can't take a step without him; we can't move!"

Mrs. Campbell: "I can't let you. Oh, isn't it horrible!"

Campbell: "Yes; a nice thing is always ten times nicer than you expected it to be!"

Mrs. Campbell: "Oh, how can you stand there mocking me? Why don't you go to him at once, and tell him the whole thing, and beg him, implore him, to help us?"

Campbell: "Why, you just told me I mustn't!"

Mrs. Campbell: "You didn't expect me to say you might, did you? Oh, how cruel!" She whirls out of the room, and Campbell stands in a daze, in which he is finally aware of Mr. Arthur Welling, seen through the open window, on the veranda without. Mr. Welling, with a terrified and furtive air, seems to be fixed to the spot where he stands.

# II

# *MR. WELLING; MR. CAMPBELL*

Campbell: "Why, Welling, what the devil are you doing there?"

Welling: "Trying to get away."

Campbell: "To get away? But you sha'n't, man! I won't let you. I was just going to see you. How long have you been there?"

Welling: "I've just come."

Campbell: "What have you heard?"

Welling: "Nothing—nothing. I was knocking on the window-casing to make *you* hear, but you seemed preoccupied."

Campbell: "Preoccupied! convulsed! cataclysmed! Look here: we're in a box, Welling. And you've got us into it." He pulls Welling's note out of his pocket, where he has been keeping his hand on it, and pokes it at him. "Is that yours?"

Welling, examining it with bewilderment mounting into anger: "It's mine; yes. May I ask, Mr. Campbell, how you came to have this letter?"

Campbell: "May I ask, Mr. Welling, how you came to write such a letter to my wife?"

Welling: "To your wife? To Mrs. Campbell? I never wrote any such letter to her."

Campbell: "Then you addressed it to her."

Welling: "Impossible!"

Campbell: "Impossible? I think I can convince you, much as I regret to do so." He makes search about Mrs. Campbell's letters on the table first, and then on the writing-desk. "We have the envelope. It came amongst a lot of letters, and there's no mistake about it." He continues to toss the letters about, and then desists. "But no matter; I can't find it; Amy's probably carried it off with her. There's no mistake about it. I was going to have some fun with you about it, but now you can have some fun with me. Whom did you send Mrs. Campbell's letter to?"

Welling: "Mrs. Campbell's letter?"

Campbell: "Oh, pshaw! your acceptance or refusal, or whatever it was, of her garden fandango. You got an invitation?"

Welling: "Of course."

Campbell: "And you wrote to accept it or decline it at the same time that you wrote this letter here to some one else. And you addressed two envelopes before you put the notes in either. And then you put them into the wrong envelopes. And you sent this note to my wife, and the other note to the other person—"

Welling: "No, I didn't do anything of the kind!" He regards Campbell with amazement, and some apparent doubt of his sanity.

Campbell: "Well, then, Mr. Welling, will you allow me to ask what the deuce you did do?"

Welling: "I never wrote to Mrs. Campbell at all. I thought I would just drop in and tell her why I couldn't come. It seemed so formal to write."

Campbell: "Then will you be kind enough to tell me whom you *did* write to?"

Welling: "No, Mr. Campbell, I can't do that."

Campbell: "You write such a letter as that to my wife, and then won't tell me whom it's to?"

Welling: "No! And you've no right to ask me."

Campbell: "I've no right to ask you?"

Welling: "No. When I tell you that the note wasn't meant for Mrs. Campbell, that's enough."

Campbell: "I'll be judge of that, Mr. Welling. You say that you were not writing two notes at the time, and that you didn't get the envelopes mixed. Then, if the note wasn't meant for my wife, why did you address it to her?"

Welling: "That's what I can't tell; that's what I don't know. It's as great a mystery to me as it is to you. I can only conjecture that when I was writing that address I was thinking of coming to explain to Mrs. Campbell that I was going away to-day, and shouldn't be back till after her party. It was too complicated to put in a note without seeming to give my regrets too much importance. And I suppose that when I was addressing the note that I did write I put Mrs. Campbell's name on because I had her so much in mind."

Campbell, with irony: "Oh!"

# III

## MRS. CAMPBELL; MR. WELLING; MR. CAMPBELL

Mrs. Campbell, appearing through the portière that separates the breakfast-room from the parlor beyond: "Yes!" She goes up and gives her hand to Mr. Welling with friendly frankness. "And it was very nice of you to think of me at such a time, when you ought to have been thinking of some one else."

Welling, with great relief and effusion: "Oh, thank you, Mrs. Campbell! I was sure you would understand. You couldn't have imagined me capable of addressing such language to you; of presuming—of—"

Mrs. Campbell: "Of course not! And Willis has quite lost his head. I saw in an instant just how it was. I'm so sorry you can't come to my party—"

Campbell: "Amy, have you been eavesdropping?"

Mrs. Campbell: "There was no need of eavesdropping. I could have heard you out at Loon Rock Light, you shouted so. But as soon as I recognized Mr. Welling's voice I came to the top of the stairs and listened. I was sure you would do something foolish. But now I think we had better make a clean breast of it, and tell Mr. Welling just what we've done. We knew, of course, the letter wasn't for me, and we thought we wouldn't vex you about it, but just send it to the one it *was* meant for. We've surprised your secret, Mr. Welling, though we didn't intend to; but if you'll accept our congratulations—under the rose, of course—we won't let it go any further. It does seem so perfectly ideal, and I feel like saying, Bless you, my children! You've been in and out here so much this summer, and I feel just like an elder sister to Margaret."

Welling: "Margaret?"

Mrs. Campbell: "Well, Miss Rice, then—"

Welling: "Miss Rice?"

Mrs. Campbell, with dignity: "Oh, I'm sorry if we seem to presume upon our acquaintance with the matter. We couldn't very well help knowing it under the circumstances."

Welling: "Certainly, certainly—of course: I don't mind that at all: I was going to tell you, anyway: that was partly the reason why I came instead of writing

—"

Campbell, in an audible soliloquy: "I supposed he *had* written."

Mrs. Campbell, intensely: "Don't interrupt, Willis! Well?"

Welling: "But I don't see what Miss Rice has to do with it."

Mrs. Campbell: "You don't see! Why, isn't Margaret Rice the one—"

Welling: "What one?"

Mrs. Campbell: "The one that you're engaged—the one that the note was really *for?*"

Welling: "No! What an idea! Miss Rice? Not for an instant! It's—it's her friend—Miss Greenway—who's staying with her—"

Mrs. Campbell, in a very awful voice: "Willis! Get me some water—some wine! Help me! Ah! Don't touch me! It was you, *you* who did it all! Oh, *now* what shall I do?" She drops her head upon Campbell's shoulder, while Welling watches them in stupefaction.

Campbell: "It's about a million times nicer than we could have expected. That's the way with a nice thing when you get it started. Well, young man, you're done for; and so are we, for that matter. We supposed that note which you addressed to Mrs. Campbell was intended for Miss Rice—"

Welling: "Ho, ho, ho! Ah, ha, ha! Miss Rice? Ha—"

Campbell: "I'm glad you like it. You'll enjoy the rest of it still better. We thought it was for Miss Rice, and my wife neatly imitated your hand on an envelope and sent it over to her just before you came in. Funny, isn't it? Laugh on! Don't mind *us!*"

Welling, aghast: "Thought my note was for Miss Rice? Sent it to her? Gracious powers!" They all stand for a moment in silence, and then Welling glances at the paper in his hand. "But there's some mistake. You haven't sent my note to Miss Rice: here it is now!"

Campbell: "Oh, that's the best of the joke. Mrs. Campbell took a copy"—Mrs. Campbell moans—"she meant to have some fun with you about it, and it's ten times as much fun as *I* expected; and in her hurry she sent off her copy and kept the original. Perhaps that makes it better."

Mrs. Campbell, detaching herself from him and confronting Mr. Welling: "No; worse! She'll think we've been trying to hoax her, and she'll be in a towering rage; and she'll show the note to Miss Greenway, and you'll be ruined. Oh poor Mr. Welling! Oh, what a fatal, fatal—mix!" She abandons herself in an attitude of extreme desperation upon a chair, while the men stare at her, till Campbell breaks the spell by starting forward and ringing the bell on the table.

Mrs. Campbell: "What are you doing, Willis?"

Campbell: "Ringing for Jane." As Jane appears: "Did you give Miss Rice the note?"

# IV

## *JANE; MRS. CAMPBELL; WELLING; CAMPBELL*

Jane: "No, sir; I gave it to the man. He said he would give it to Miss Rice."

Campbell: "Then it's all up. If by any chance she hadn't got it, Amy, you might have sent over for it, and said there was a mistake."

Jane: "He said Miss Rice was out driving with Miss Greenway in her phaeton, but they expected her back every minute."

Mrs. Campbell: "Oh, my goodness! And you didn't come to tell me? Oh, if we had only known! We've lost our only chance, Willis."

Jane: "I did come and knock on your door, ma'am, but I couldn't make you hear."

Campbell: "There's still a chance. Perhaps she hasn't got back yet."

Jane: "I know she ain't, sir. I've been watching for her ever since. I can always see them come, from the pantry window."

Mrs. Campbell: "Well, then, don't stand there talking, but run at once! Oh, Willis! Never tell me again that there's no such thing as an overruling providence. Oh, what an interposition! Oh, I can never be grateful and humble enough—Goodness me, Jane! why don't you go?"

Jane: "Go where, ma'am? I don't know what you want me to do. I'm willing enough to do anything if I know what it is, but it's pretty hard to do things if you don't."

Campbell: "You're perfectly right, Jane. Mrs. Campbell wants you to telegraph yourself over to Mrs. Rice's, and say to her that the letter you left for Miss Rice is not for her, but another lady, and Mrs. Campbell sent it by mistake. Get it and bring it back here, dead or alive, even if Mrs. Rice has to pass over your mangled body in the attempt."

Jane, tasting the joke, while Mrs. Campbell gasps in ineffective efforts to reinforce her husband's instructions: "I will that, sir."

# V

## *MRS. CAMPBELL; WELLING; CAMPBELL*

Campbell: "And now, while we're waiting, let's all join hands and dance round the table. You're saved, Welling. So are you, Amy. And so am I— which is more to the point."

Mrs. Campbell, gayly: "Dansons!" She extends her hands to the gentlemen, and as they circle round the breakfast-table she sings,

*"Sur le pont d'Avignon,*
*Tout le monde y danse en rond."*

She frees her hands and courtesies to one gentleman and the other.

*"Les belles dames font comme ça;*
*Les beaux messieurs font comme ça."*

Then she catches hands with them again, and they circle round the table as before, singing,

*"Sur le pont d'Avignon,*
*Tout le monde y danse en rond.*

Oh, dear! Stop! I'm dizzy—I shall fall." She spins into a chair, while the men continue solemnly circling by themselves.

Campbell: "It is a sacred dance:

*"Sur le pont d'Avignon—"*

Welling: "It's an expiation:

*"Tout le monde y danse en rond."*

Mrs. Campbell, springing from her chair and running to the window: "Stop, you crazy things! Here comes Jane! Come right in here, Jane! Did you get it? Give it to me, Jane!"

Welling: "*I* think it belongs to me, Mrs. Campbell."

Campbell: "Jane, I am master of the house—nominally. Give me the letter."

# VI

## *JANE; MRS. CAMPBELL; WELLING; CAMPBELL*

Jane, entering, blown and panting, through the open window: "Oh, how I did run—"

Mrs. Campbell: "Yes, yes! But the letter—"

Welling: "Did you get it?"

Campbell: "Where is it?"

Jane, fanning herself with her apron: "I can't hardly get my breath—"

Mrs. Campbell: "Had she got back?"

Jane: "No, ma'am."

Campbell: "Did Mrs. Rice object to giving it up?"

Jane: "No, sir."

Welling: "Then it's all right?"

Jane: "No, sir. All wrong."

Welling: "All wrong?"

Campbell: "How all wrong?"

Mrs. Campbell: "What's all wrong, Jane?"

Jane: "Please, ma'am, may I have a drink of water? I'm so dry I can't speak."

Mrs. Campbell: "Yes, certainly."

Campbell: "Of course."

Welling: "Here." They all pour glasses of water and press them to her lips.

Jane, pushing the glasses away, and escaping from the room: "They thought Mrs. Campbell was in a great hurry for Miss Rice to have the letter, and they sent off the man with it to meet her."

---

# VII

## *MRS. CAMPBELL; WELLING; CAMPBELL*

Mrs. Campbell: "Oh, merciful goodness!"

Welling: "Gracious powers!"

Campbell: "Another overruling providence. Now you *are* in for it, my boy! So is Amy. And so am I—which is still more to the point."

Mrs. Campbell: "Well, now, what shall we do?"

Campbell: "All that we can do now is to await developments: they'll come fast enough. Miss Rice will open her letter as soon as she gets it, and she won't understand it in the least; how *could* she understand a letter in your handwriting, with Welling's name signed to it? She'll show it to Miss Greenway—"

Welling: "Oh, don't say that!"

Campbell: "—Greenway; and Miss Greenway won't know what to make of it either. But she's the kind of girl who'll form some lively conjectures when she reads that letter. In the first place, she'll wonder how Mr. Welling happens to be writing to Miss Rice in that affectionate strain—"

Mrs. Campbell, in an appealing shriek: "Willis!"

Campbell: "—And she naturally won't believe he's done it. But then, when Miss Rice tells her it's your handwriting, Amy, she'll think that you and Miss Rice have been having your jokes about Mr. Welling; and she'll wonder what kind of person you are, anyway, to make free with a young man's name that way."

Welling: "Oh, I assure you that she admires Mrs. Campbell more than anybody."

Mrs. Campbell: "Don't try to stop him; he's fiendish when he begins teasing."

Campbell: "Oh, well! If she admires Mrs. Campbell and confides in you, then the whole affair is very simple. All you've got to do is to tell her that after you'd written her the original of that note, your mind was so full of Mrs. Campbell and her garden-party that you naturally addressed it to her. And then Mrs. Campbell can cut in and say that when she got the note she knew it wasn't for her, but she never dreamed of your caring for Miss Greenway, and was so sure it was for Miss Rice that she sent her a copy of it. That will make it all right and perfectly agreeable to every one concerned."

Mrs. Campbell: "And I can say that I sent it at your suggestion, and then, instead of trying to help me out of the awful, awful—box, you took a cruel pleasure in teasing me about it! But I shall not say anything, for I shall not see them. I will leave you to receive them and make the best of it. Don't *try* to stop me, Willis." She threatens him with her fan as he steps forward to intercept her escape.

Campbell: "No, no! Listen, Amy! You *must* stay and see those ladies. It's all well enough to leave it to me, but what about poor Welling? *He* hasn't done anything—except cause the whole trouble."

Mrs. Campbell: "I am very sorry, but I can't help it. I must go." Campbell continues to prevent her flight, and she suddenly whirls about and makes a dash at the open window. "Oh, very well, then! I can get out this way." At the same moment Miss Rice and Miss Greenway appear before the window on the piazza. "Ugh! E—e—e! How you frightened me! But—but come in. So gl —glad to see you! And you—you too, Miss Greenway. Here's Mr. Welling. He's been desolating us with a story about having to be away over my party, and just getting back for Mrs. Curwen's. Isn't it too bad? Can't some of you young ladies—or all of you—make him stay?" As Mrs. Campbell talks on, she readjusts her spirit more and more to the exigency, and subdues her agitation to a surface of the sweetest politeness.

---

# VIII

## *MISS RICE, MISS GREENWAY, and the OTHERS*

Miss Rice, entering with an unopened letter in her hand, which she extends to Mrs. Campbell: "What in the world does it all mean, Mrs. Campbell, your sending your letters flying after *me* at this rate?"

Mrs. Campbell, with a gasp: "My letters?" She mechanically receives the extended note, and glances at the superscription: "*Mrs. Willis Campbell*. Ah!" She hands it quickly to her husband, who reads the address with a similar cry.

Campbell: "Well, well, Amy! This is a pretty good joke on you. You've sealed up one of your own notes, and sent it to Miss Rice. Capital! Ah, ha, ha!"

Mrs. Campbell, with hysterical rapture: "Oh, how delicious! What a ridiculous blunder! I don't wonder you were puzzled, Margaret."

Welling: "What! Sent her your own letter, addressed to yourself?"

Mrs. Campbell: "Yes. Isn't it amusing?"

Welling: "The best thing I ever heard of."

Miss Rice: "Yes. And if you only knew what agonies of curiosity Miss Greenway and I had suffered, wanting to open it and read it anyway, in spite of all the decencies, I think you would read it to us."

Campbell: "Or at least give Miss Rice her own letter. What in the world did you do with that?"

Mrs. Campbell: "Put it in my desk, where I thought I put mine. But never mind it now. I can tell you what was in it just as well. Come in here a moment, Margaret." She leads the way to the parlor, whither Miss Rice follows.

Miss Greenway, poutingly: "Oh, mayn't I know, too? I think that's hardly fair, Mrs. Campbell."

Mrs. Campbell: "No; or—Margaret may tell you afterwards; or Mr. Welling may, *now!*"

Miss Greenway: "How very formidable!"

Mrs. Campbell, over her shoulder, on going out: "Willis, bring me the refusals and acceptances, won't you? They're up-stairs."

Campbell: "Delighted to be of any service." Behind Miss Greenway's back he dramatizes over her head to Welling his sense of his own escape, and his compassion for the fellow-man whom he leaves in the toils of fate.

# IX

## *MISS GREENWAY; MR. WELLING*

Welling: "Nelly!" He approaches, and timidly takes her hand.

Miss Greenway: "Arthur! That letter was addressed in your handwriting. Will you please explain?"

Welling: "Why, it's very simple—that is, it's the most difficult thing in the world. Nelly, can you believe *any*thing I say to you?"

Miss Greenway: "What nonsense! Of course I can—if you're not too long about it."

Welling: "Well, then, the letter in that envelope was one I wrote to Mrs. Campbell—or the copy of one."

Miss Greenway: "The copy?"

Welling: "But let me explain. You see, when I got your note asking me to be sure and come to Mrs. Curwen's—"

Miss Greenway: "Yes?"

Welling: "—I had just received an invitation from Mrs. Campbell for her garden-party, and I sat down and wrote to you, and concluded I'd step over and tell her why I couldn't come, and with that in mind I addressed your letter —the one I'd written you—to her."

Miss Greenway: "With my name inside?"

Welling: "No; I merely called you 'darling'; and when Mrs. Campbell opened it she saw it couldn't be for her, and she took it into her head it must be for Miss Rice."

Miss Greenway: "For Margaret? What an idea! But why did she put your envelope on it?"

Welling: "She made a copy, for the joke of it; and then, in her hurry, she enclosed that in my envelope, and kept the original and the envelope she'd addressed to Miss Rice, and—and that's all."

Miss Greenway: "What a perfectly delightful muddle! And how shall we get out of it with Margaret?"

Welling: "With Margaret? I don't care for her. It's you that I want to get out of it with. And you do believe me—you do forgive me, Nelly?"

Miss Greenway: "For what?"

Welling: "For—for—I don't know what for. But I thought you'd be so vexed."

Miss Greenway: "I shouldn't have liked you to send a letter addressed darling to Mrs. Curwen; but Mrs. Campbell is different."

Welling: "Oh, how archangelically sensible! How divine of you to take it in just the right way!"

**MR. WELLING EXPLAINS.**

Miss Greenway: "Why, of course! How stupid I should be to take such a thing in the wrong way!"

Welling: "And I'm so glad now I didn't try to lie to you about it."

Miss Greenway: "It wouldn't have been of any use. You couldn't have carried off anything of that sort. The truth is bad enough for *you* to carry off. Promise me that you will always leave the other thing to *me*."

Welling: "I will, darling; I will, indeed."

Miss Greenway: "And now we must tell Margaret, of course."

# X

## *MISS RICE; then MR. and MRS. CAMPBELL, and the OTHERS*

Miss Rice, rushing in upon them, and clasping Miss Greenway in a fond embrace: "You needn't. Mrs. Campbell has told me; and oh, Nelly, I'm so happy for you! And isn't it all the greatest mix?"

Campbell, rushing in, and wringing Welling's hand: "You needn't tell me, either; I've been listening, and I've heard every word. I congratulate you, my dear boy! I'd no idea she'd let you up so easily. You'll allow yourself it isn't a very likely story."

Welling: "I know it. But—"

Miss Rice: "That's the very reason no one could have made it up."

Miss Greenway: "*He* couldn't have made up even a likely story."

Campbell: "Congratulate you again, Welling. Do you suppose she can keep so always?"

Mrs. Campbell, rushing in with extended hands: "Don't answer the wretch, Mr. Welling. Of course she can with *you*. Dansons!" She gives a hand to Miss Greenway and Welling each; the others join them, and as they circle round the table she sings,

> *"Sur le pont d'Avignon,*
> *Tout le monde y danse en rond."*

### THE END